THIS BOOK BELONGS TO

PETTICOAT PIRATES

The Mermaids of Starfish Reef

The Sea Fairies of Whirlpool Gully

The Seahorses of Scallop Bay

Petticoat
PIRATES

The Sea Fairies
of Whirlpool Gully

ERICA-JANE WATERS

LITTLE, BROWN BOOKS FOR YOUNG READERS
lbkids.co.uk

LITTLE, BROWN BOOKS FOR YOUNG READERS

First published in Great Britain in 2013 by Little, Brown Books for Young Readers

A CIP catalogue record for this book
is available from the British Library.

ISBN 978-1-907411-97-7

Typeset in Golden Cockerel by M Rules
Printed and bound in Great Britain by
Clays, St Ives plc

Papers used by LBYR are from well-managed forests
and other responsible sources.

MIX
Paper from
responsible sources
FSC www.fsc.org   FSC® C104740

Little, Brown Books for Young Readers
An imprint of
Little, Brown Book Group
100 Victoria Embankment
London EC4Y 0DY

An Hachette UK Company
www.hachette.co.uk

www.lbkids.co.uk

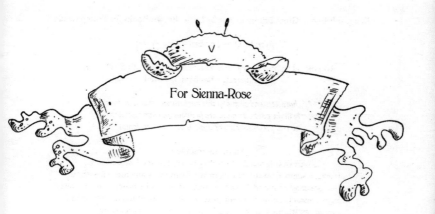

For Sienna-Rose

SCALLOP BAY

STARFISH REEF

RAZOR BAY

WHIRLPOOL GULLY

PERIWINKLE
LAGOON
AND THE SURROUNDING
SEAS

THE
PETTICOAT PIRATES

PERIWINKLE LAGOON

Contents

Prologue

It was a summer morn when a little basket floated into Periwinkle Lagoon. Inside were three beautiful baby girls, shaded by a tattered umbrella.

From that moment on, the ruler of the lagoon, Captainess Periwinkle, raised the three girls as her own. She named them Marina, Aqua and Oceana.

Marina loved studying the maps in the flagship drawing room and amazed the

Captainess with her accurate drawing skills.
Marina's first words were in Mer, a language
in which she was mysteriously fluent, and she
seemed to be able to listen to the wind, as
though it were telling her something.

Aqua loved dressing up in the Captainess's frilly skirts and sparkling necklaces. She would spend hours rummaging through jewellery boxes and treasure chests full of pearls. When Aqua was tiny, she wouldn't ask for bedtime stories about princesses or fairies – she wanted to hear about the monsters and beasties of the deep, deep seas.

Oceana loved the flagship library where the walls were covered with oil paintings of every type of pirate ship. As soon as she could read, she spent her time learning how to build ships and studying the way that things were put together. Captainess Periwinkle gave her a microscope as a birthday present and Oceana

was amazed at how different seaweed looked really close up.

The years passed until the girls were old enough to live on their own ship, *The Petticoat*, and the girls became known as the Petticoat Pirates.

Chapter One

Marina stretched and yawned as the bright summer sun shone through her porthole window and on to her bunk bed. She climbed down her ladder, walked over the warm wooden boards of her cabin and made her way up on to *The Petticoat*'s deck.

This was a busy time of year at Periwinkle Lagoon. All the pirates were preparing for the Midsummer Fair. Everyone from pirates to sea fairies and mermaids gathered every summer at

the lagoon for the grand fair where they could buy their favourite things.

As Marina felt the warm sea breeze ruffling her long nightgown, she watched many, many ships and boats making their way back into the lagoon after long fishing trips or harvesting delicious sea crops.

"You're up late this morn!" came a chirpy voice. It was Aqua, holding a tray with three tall glasses and a jug containing sparkly pink juice. "I've been in the cabin making a fresh batch of sea strawberry juice while you were still in your bunk."

"Oh, delicious," Marina said, reaching for a glass of the refreshing drink. "Where's Oceana, is she below deck too?"

"No, my sleepy little starfish, she was up before the sun. We heard that a boat had arrived back from its long trip to Sea Crystal Cove. She wanted to try and buy a bag of sea crystal sugar for us to sprinkle on our kelp flakes!"

"I hope she's not too much longer," giggled Marina. "My tummy is rumbling like a whale in a whirlpool!"

The girls' laughter was interrupted by a clatter and a thud.

"Oh, limpets," Oceana groaned. She had dropped her shopping as she climbed on to the deck of *The Petticoat*. Now there were pink and white granules everywhere! Oceana was extremely clumsy but her kind heart and her clever mind more than made up for the odd spillage.

"Here, let us help you," Marina said,

kneeling down next to Aqua to help scoop up the sea crystals and place them back in their little paper bag.

"Oh, limpets, it just slipped right out of my arms," Oceana said, looking at her hands and then down at her two friends happily clearing up the mess.

"Don't be silly, we all drop things now and then," Aqua said, putting her arm around Oceana.

"And besides," added Marina, "we wouldn't have anything to sprinkle on our kelp flakes at all without you! Thank you for getting up early so we had something to cheer up our breakfast."

"Well, I could only buy one bag. The crystal merchants want to save the rest for the fair."

"I'm so excited about the Midsummer fair," Marina said. "There are going to be so many exotic things to stock up on!"

"I heard that the sea lace fairies will be there again," gushed Aqua. "I bought the most beautiful dress from their stall last year."

Aqua disappeared back into *The Petticoat*'s cabin to fetch three bowls of kelp flakes while Oceana placed the little bag of sea crystal sugar on the table.

"Aqua certainly knows how to look after us," Oceana said as she sat down at the beautifully laid-out table on the deck and sipped her sea strawberry juice. "Are you OK, Marina? You look a little worried."

Marina was staring out over the lagoon. The sun was making the sea sparkle and the summer sea birds were happily tweeting away

on the mast of the ship. But something in the wind told Marina that trouble was coming.

"I think we should go inside," Marina said. She spun around so fast she spilled her strawberry juice over her nightgown.

"Why, whatever's the matter?" asked Oceana.

"It's the wind – but there's no time to talk," Marina said. She quickly ushered Oceana into the cabin and locked the heavy wooden door with its large iron key.

"What on earth is going on?" asked Aqua as her two friends rushed around, closing all the portholes.

"The wind has warned Marina about something," gasped Oceana.

"Your friend the wind can be very vague," Aqua tutted whilst pouring herself a bowl of sea

13

kelp flakes. "Did you bring the sea crystal sugar in with you?"

"This is no time to be worrying about breakfast!" Marina cried, and then pointed out of one of the portholes. "Look, over there!"

The three pirates peered out.

"What is that?" asked Oceana. "It looks like a bluey-green cloud."

"That's no cloud," Marina shuddered.

"Sea fairies!" Aqua shrieked. "And they don't look like friendly ones!"

Marina, Aqua and Oceana looked on as the swarm of little fairies flitted and fluttered from ship to ship around the lagoon.

"What are they doing?" Oceana whispered.

"I'm not sure, but they don't look very happy," said Marina.

Slowly but steadily the blue and green fairies moved closer to *The Petticoat*, and as they did so the girls could see that the little creatures were sprinkling glittering powder over all the pirate ships in the lagoon.

"Oh, limpets," said Oceana, "every ship on the lagoon will have its portholes and doors open on such a warm day as this! Whatever that glittering powder is, I'm sure it's not going to do anyone any good!"

The Petticoat Pirates stepped back with a jolt as two little fairies, one blue and one green, began circling the ship, their sparkling wings glistening in the sunlight.

"They're looking for a way in," whispered Marina. "Thank goodness we closed all the portholes."

"We did," muttered a pale Aqua, "all except that one!"

The girls' gazes followed Aqua's pointed finger – the two cross-looking little sea fairies held up their arms, ready to throw their fairy powder.

"Quick," hissed Aqua, "hold your noses. Sea fairies' spells are powerless if you hold your breath!"

A sea of blue and green glittering powder rained through the porthole and down upon the girls as they held their noses as tightly as they could.

Then the sea fairies were gone from *The Petticoat*, and the three girls unclasped their noses and gasped for air.

"Have they gone?" asked Oceana.

"They have," replied Marina, who'd seen the mass of green and blue leave the lagoon just moments before, "but it's what they've left behind that I'm concerned about!"

Cautiously the girls unlocked the great wooden door of the cabin and stepped back out on to the deck.

"At least they didn't pinch our sea crystal sugar," Aqua smiled as she picked up the little bag of sweetness. But Marina was looking out to the wide lagoon, her face anxious.

"Oceana, can I borrow your telescope please?" she asked.

"I'll fetch it," replied Oceana as she hurried down the hatch in the main deck floor to the cabins below.

"There's something very strange going on," Marina said, squinting her eyes in the strong summer light.

"Here you are, Marina." Oceana passed her the telescope.

"Bubbles!" exclaimed Marina.

"Bubbles?" Aqua and Oceana said in unison.

"Every pirate in Periwinkle Lagoon is hiccupping bubbles. Blue and green bubbles!"

Chapter Two

A bubbly, hiccupping panic had broken out in the lagoon. Pirates were clambering into their rowing boats and frantically making their way over to the flagship to see Captainess Periwinkle. In their rush, some pirates had jumped straight into the sea and were swimming over, hiccupping bubbles as they went.

Marina and her friends watched as the lagoon frothed with rowing boats and splashing

pirates, the odd lost wooden leg bobbing along in the blue water.

"Aqua and I should get dressed then we'll all row over to the flagship too," Marina said to Oceana. "By the time we're ready hopefully the rush will have quieted down."

Within minutes all three girls were dressed in their pretty petticoats, the buttons on their blouses fastened and their boots and shoes buckled and tied.

"Are we ready, girls?" Marina called from her cabin as she combed her long inky hair and straightened her little black hat.

"Coming! I'm just looking for my blue and green pearls – those fairies have given me a flash of fashion inspiration," Aqua called back.

"What about you, Oceana?" Marina popped her head around the door to Oceana's cabin,

admiring her neat rows of potions, test tubes and jars that lined the shelves.

"Oh, I'm ready, I just want to bring some sample jars," Oceana said as she popped a few green bottles with cork stoppers into her bag.

"Good thinking," Marina said. "I'm sure Captainess Periwinkle will want us to examine the bubbles to try and figure out where those fairies came from."

"Are you two coming?" Aqua shouted as she climbed the ladder up to the main deck. Marina and Oceana followed quickly behind and then the girls clambered down the hull of *The Petticoat* and into their little rowing boat.

"Eyepatches on, pirates," Marina said as she

took the oars. "Let's go and see what we can do to help."

The deck of the flagship was heaving with hiccupping pirates and bubbles.

"It's a curse!" one pirate shouted.

"We're doomed!" cried another.

"It's the end ... hic ... of Peri ... hic ... winkle lagoon as we know it!" hiccupped a third.

By the time the girls had made their way towards the poop deck, they were covered in green and blue slime where the bubbles had been bursting around them.

"This stuff is as sticky as a sticklefish!" Aqua groaned, scraping some of the slime off her blouse with a hairclip.

"I'll have that," said Oceana, holding out her little glass sample jar.

Aqua plopped the bluey-green gloop from her clip into the jar and Oceana sealed it with the cork stopper.

"I can examine this under my microscope when I get back to my cabin," Oceana said, putting the jar up to the sun.

"Listen," whispered Marina, "I think I can hear Captainess Periwinkle."

A hiccupping hush fell over the ship as Captainess Periwinkle appeared above them on the poop deck.

"Pirates," she hollered, popping several bubbles with her sword, "we have found ourselves in a very sticky ... hic ... situation."

"Oh no," said Marina. "Even Captainess Periwinkle has the hiccups!"

"You will no doubt ... hic ... have seen an angry swarm of sea fairies in the lagoon

this morn. They left no ship untouched and we have all been ... hic ... cursed!"

Marina, Aqua and Oceana all looked at one another, wondering when would be a good time to mention that they had escaped it.

"This is ... hic ... terrible news for the Midsummer Fair," the Captainess continued. "No one will come near the lagoon if word spreads of a ... hic ... fairy curse!" The Captainess popped

several more bubbles with her sword as the pirates erupted into a frenzy.

"How am I going to decorate my ... hic ... cakes?" the pirate from the Periwinkle Bakery cried, wringing his white apron between his hands. "I buy coral sparkles ... hic ... every year at the fair!"

"And I've made ... hic ... five-hundred spicy sea-slug sausages!" cried a butcher pirate. "How am I going to sell them all?"

Marina took her friends' hands and stepped forward out of the crowd.

"Marina," called Captainess Periwinkle, noticing the Petticoat Pirates at once, "did you have something you wanted . . . hic . . . to say? Come hither."

Marina led Aqua and Oceana up the wooden steps to the poop deck where Captainess Periwinkle was waiting for them.

Standing next to the Captainess, Marina began to speak to the pirates below.

"Captainess and pirates of Periwinkle Lagoon – we think we may be able to help."

"Why aren't you . . . hic . . . hiccupping?" asked one of the pirates as an enormous blue bubble emerged from his mouth.

Marina gestured towards Aqua. "Aqua knew that if we held our breath, the fairy curse would not affect us, so we escaped the hiccups," she said.

29

"Oh, my beautiful little Petticoat...
hic... Pirates," gurgled Captainess Periwinkle,
popping one of her bubbles with her finger, "I
was hoping you would be able to help. Tell us,
what is your... hic... plan?"

"Well," continued Marina, "we don't have a
plan as such, but we'll take this bubble slime sample
back to *The Petticoat* and see what we can do."

The girls left Captainess Periwinkle trying
to calm the hiccupping crowd and slipped
back to *The Petticoat* where they headed straight
below deck to Oceana's cabin.

The girls huddled around Oceana's desk.
There were rows of test tubes full of brilliantly
coloured powders, all neatly labelled with little
pink stickers, and Petri dishes with strange
furry balls growing inside. In the middle of the
table was Oceana's microscope.

Oceana poured some of the bubble slime from her sample jar on to a little glass plate, and then slid it under the microscope.

"Interesting, very interesting," Oceana whispered under her breath, her right eye pressed firmly to the microscope viewer.

"What! What's interesting?" Aqua asked impatiently.

"Aqua, would you mind closing my

porthole curtains, please? I think I know what this is."

Aqua pulled the little curtains and the cabin fell into darkness.

"Yes! I knew it!" cried Oceana.

Marina leant closer to the microscope. "What is it, Oceana?"

"Look closely," said Oceana, moving back so her friends could get near.

There, under the microscope, the bubble slime glowed like a million little stars, sparkling blue and green. Marina and then Aqua took turns to look, and were both transfixed.

"That's the prettiest slime I've ever seen," murmured Aqua. "What is it?"

"It looks and smells like blue branching seaweed, but there's something else mixed in with it too that's causing it to glow blue and

green," replied Oceana. "I think it's some sort of clam or shellfish."

Suddenly Aqua leapt up and ran next door into her cabin, returning a moment later with a thick book trimmed with seashells.

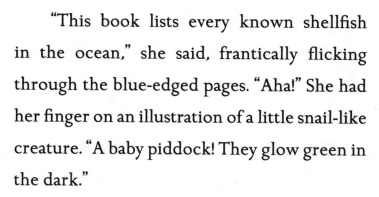

"This book lists every known shellfish in the ocean," she said, frantically flicking through the blue-edged pages. "Aha!" She had her finger on an illustration of a little snail-like creature. "A baby piddock! They glow green in the dark."

"Baby piddocks? I saw some baskets of freshly harvested baby piddocks arriving on one of the fishing boats yesterday evening," Marina said, her voice high with concern. "I noticed

because they're so rare. I've never seen them here at the lagoon before."

"They only grow around the rocks at Whirlpool Gully. But there's a rumour that we must never remove them from the rocks," Aqua replied. "I'm surprised they've been harvested."

"But why would anyone go near there anyway?" asked Marina. "Whirlpool Gully is so dangerous!" She'd heard that the biggest whirlpool, Old Inky, could even suck a whole ship down into its swirling darkness.

"The pirates on the fishing boat that harvested the baby piddocks must have been very brave," added Oceana.

"Or very silly!" said Aqua. "There's a huge sea fairy colony at Whirlpool Gully. I bet they are the fairies that visited us this

morn – and they are angry because someone from Periwinkle Lagoon has taken their baby piddocks!"

"Then we must take them back!" Marina said, standing up and walking towards Oceana's cabin door. "Perhaps then the fairies will lift their curse."

"You mean we have to go to Whirl… Whirl… Whirlpool Gully?" quivered Oceana. "Whirlpool Gully, home of Old Inky? In *The Petticoat*?"

"Don't be afraid, my little catfish," Aqua said, putting an arm around her timid friend. "You're forgetting that Marina is a master map reader – she will guide us safely. She would never let us get close enough to Old Inky to be in any danger."

Marina was busy writing a note with a

seagull feather quill pen, which she handed to Oceana.

"Here, go and give this to Captainess Periwinkle. Aqua, can you go and collect those baby piddocks? I'll set the course for our journey and ready the ship."

Less than an hour later the three pirates had hoisted the sails of *The Petticoat*, lifted the anchor and set off to find the sea fairies of Whirlpool Gully.

Chapter Three

Sailing through the warm western seas, *The Petticoat*'s pink sails flapped in the breeze. Blue flying fish with little rosy bellies jumped through the waves alongside the bow of the ship as it made its way towards Whirlpool Gully.

"Look, up there!" cried Marina, pointing at the sky.

The girls watched as

a flock of bright peach and pink flamingos flew past them and on to the mangrove swamps at Sea Serpent Bay.

"The western seas are so, so beautiful at this time of year," sighed Marina as she turned the ship's wheel to keep them on course.

"The warm sea air's making me thirsty," Aqua said, smacking her lips. "I know, I've got just the thing for three thirsty pirate girls." She disappeared into the cabin and returned moments later with three glasses of sparkling sea lemonade.

"Mmm, delicious," said Marina, sipping her drink. "Oceana, would you mind taking the wheel for a moment while I study the map?"

"Aye, aye, Captain!" replied Oceana enthusiastically as she jumped to the helm.

Marina unrolled the map on a little

wooden table on the main deck of *The Petticoat*.
She sat down with Aqua and placed seashells on
the corners to stop the map blowing away in the
breeze.

"I can't see the sea fairy colony anywhere
on this map," Marina sighed.

"Ah," said Aqua, "I've been looking through

my book, *Sea Fairies of the Western Seas*, and it says that the sea fairies of Whirlpool Gully live beneath the ocean!"

"But how do they breathe?" asked Marina. "I always thought sea fairies breathed air, like we do."

"You're right, my little sea kitten, they do need air," Aqua continued. "The book says they live in an underwater glass dome right beneath Old Inky itself! They are experts in ocean remedies and sea-herbal potions. But they are also secretive and mischievous, well known for casting spells and curses on unsuspecting pirates."

"As we well know!" Oceana shouted down from the poop deck.

"So how do we get into the dome?" Marina asked. "And how are the fairies going to react when we arrive?"

"That's the tricky part," Aqua replied, sucking her breath through her teeth. "Some say Old Inky is there to protect the sea fairies from visitors, and there is no written record of anyone ever having been there, well, at least—"

"What?" Oceana shouted again from above.

"Go on, Aqua, what?" whispered Marina, so as not to terrify poor Oceana even more.

"They say," continued Aqua, "that some people have tried to visit, but no one has EVER returned."

Marina's face turned whiter than a beluga whale.

"There is one thing that we MUST remember when we enter a sea fairy realm," Aqua said as she took Marina by the hand and led her up to join Oceana on the poop deck.

Marina and Oceana listened intently.

41

"Never, and I mean NEVER EVER, eat any food or drink that they offer you," Aqua said, a very serious expression on her face. "If you let even a morsel of sea fairy food pass your pretty lips, you'll be trapped in their underwater world for ever!"

The girls fell silent for several moments before Marina suddenly snapped them out of their sea fairy dream.

"Look! Straight ahead – it's Whirlpool Gully!" Marina cried. "But I think it's getting too late in the day to carry on now. Let's anchor here for the night and explore it at first light."

Marina took over the wheel as Aqua sank the anchor and Oceana tied up and secured the sails.

"It's so warm this evening," Oceana said as she climbed down from the rigging. "Why don't we sleep up on deck tonight?"

42

"Good plan," Marina replied. "Aqua, could you fetch the hammocks from the storeroom, please?"

"I'm on my way!" Aqua said as she skipped down below deck.

Before long the three girls were swaying gently in their hammocks under the stars. There was no noise apart from the creaking of *The Petticoat*'s wooden hull and the faint rumble of Old Inky in the distance.

As Marina's big green eyes began to close she sensed a faint whisper on the wind. But Marina was too sleepy from a long day of sailing to pay attention. She was soon fast asleep beneath the moon, unaware of what was bubbling up in the night sky above her.

Chapter Four

As the night turned into a blustery morning the Petticoat Pirates were awoken by a loud crackle of thunder and large raindrops plopping down on their faces. The sky was black and stormy and the dark waves were getting bigger and bigger.

Marina and Aqua jumped out of their hammocks, rubbing their eyes, while Oceana became entangled in hers and was dangling like a lobster caught in a net.

"Oh, limpets!" she wailed as her two friends helped release her.

Marina looked overboard – the seas around them were growing even higher!

"Quick, we need to raise the anchor before the line snaps!" Marina shouted, her wet hair stuck to her face.

Aqua struggled with the mechanism to hoist the anchor but soon realised it was too

late. The rudder had snapped in the huge swell and the anchor line was broken. What's more, as the lightning flashed they could see they were right on top of a huge black wave. The next moment they crested the wave and were plunged downward. *The Petticoat* was adrift and heading straight towards Whirlpool Gully!

"We're going to be sucked down Old Inky!" shrieked Oceana, clutching on to the mast and struggling to see through her wet glasses.

"We still have time to steer ourselves away, don't we?" cried Aqua.

"We can't!" shouted Marina over the thunder claps. "The rudder is broken – we have no control over the ship."

"Then I'll hoist up the sails!" Aqua began to climb the rigging and untie the soggy sails.

"No, Aqua, don't!" Marina tried desperately to make herself heard over the storm. "You'll only send us towards Whirlpool Gully faster – the wind is blowing the wrong way! We'll be blown straight down into Old Inky!"

But Aqua couldn't hear her friend's pleas, and continued to release the sails. Marina ran over to the mast where Oceana was still clinging, her eyes closed tight in terror.

Sure enough, *The Petticoat* was swept by mountainous waves directly into Whirlpool Gully. The little ship began to move in wide circles as it was caught in the current of Old Inky. Round and round it went until they were spinning so fast everything became a blur of sea and waves and walls of water.

There was a loud sucking noise and the wooden boards of *The Petticoat* groaned under

the pressure of the great whirlpool. Marina looked around and realised they were deep in the whirlpool now. She could see fish and seahorses, long lost pirate ships and treasure all spinning in the water around her. Then suddenly *The Petticoat* was sucked in completely and then spat out of the bottom of the whirlpool with a loud *splosh*!

"Oh, limpets. Have we perished?" Oceana managed to whimper.

"No! But I think we've found our way into the sea fairy realm!" Marina said, looking around at what seemed to be an under-the-sea cave. She jumped down from *The Petticoat* into the waist-high water, and gazed at the whirlpool hovering like a watery tornado above her head. "This is truly a magical place!" she added.

"Well, we may have arrived in the sea fairy

realm, but I'm yet to spot a fairy!" Aqua blurted out, her hands on her hips.

"Petticoat Pirates, look over there," Oceana said quietly, pointing towards the little sandy beach at the edge of the water.

Hundreds upon hundreds of tiny little pink crabs were scuttling up the beach from the water.

"They're everywhere!" Aqua gasped, looking down through the water at her boots, which were being trod upon by several of the crabs.

"What are they doing?" Oceana asked as she watched the little creatures, each with a small bundle of seaweed on its back.

"They must be carrier crabs," replied Aqua. "The sea fairies use them to gather seaweeds, herbs and sea flora for potions and remedies. The fairies themselves can't breathe underwater so they use these little guys to help."

Aqua leant down and picked up one of the little pink crabs.

"Hello there, me hearty. What's that you've got on your back?"

The little crab wiggled his tiny pink pincers at Aqua.

"I think he wants you to put him back down," laughed Marina.

"They all seem to be going in the same direction. If we follow them they might lead us to the sea fairies!" Oceana said.

"Good idea," replied Marina.

The three pirates gathered their baskets

of piddocks before wading towards the sandy beach. They began to follow the crabs through a network of damp tunnels, their path lit by glowing starfish that were stuck all over the walls. The tiny carrier crabs scuttled along in front, carrying their sprigs of seaweed and other sea plants.

Soon, beautiful music began to dance around the girls' ears and as they reached the end of the tunnels the most wondrous sight met their eyes.

Chapter Five

Chapter Five

"Jumping jellyfish!" Aqua muttered, her mouth wide open.

"Limpets," squeaked Oceana.

"So this is the sea fairy realm underneath Whirlpool Gully," said Marina as she peered up at the huge glass dome above their heads. She could see they were deep beneath the surface, and through the ceiling she could make out the swirls of the whirlpools above them. The beautiful dome was built on top of a natural

circle of rocks and encased the lushest garden the girls had ever seen.

They spotted fairies of all different kinds living under the dome. Some were small and flitted around the tall fruit trees that grew in the centre. Others were as big as the Petticoat Pirates and wore beautiful sparkling dresses made from delicate fish scales and deep-sea diamonds. Some had green skin, some had blue, but most were as pale as oyster shells, and they were all covered in a beautiful shimmer.

Marina and her two friends exited the tunnel and walked nervously out into the underwater dome.

"These fairies don't seem angry at all," Marina said quietly. "If anything they seem quite pleased to see us!"

A beautiful sea fairy wearing a floaty dress

trimmed with tiny flecks of coral offered them a basket of sea berries.

"Ooh, delicious," Oceana gushed, reaching for one of the juicy purple berries.

"NO!" Aqua knocked Oceana's hand away from the fairy food. "Remember what I said about not eating anything the sea fairies offer you?"

"Oh yes, I forgot," Oceana said, blushing. "Sorry."

"Look at all these wonderful shops and stalls!" gasped Marina. She wasn't sure where to look first.

"HATS! TIARAS! CROWNS!" shrieked Aqua as she pulled her two friends over to one.

The sea fairy at the stall was fastening a sea flora headpiece to her long, red hair as the girls arrived.

"These are incredible – I've never seen anything so gorgeous! May I try one?" Aqua asked the sea fairy.

"You may try on whatever you wish," she replied.

Aqua chose a tiara made from pure white coral, adorned with pink starfish.

"Oh, Aqua, you look gorgeous!" said Marina. "You must buy it."

"I mustn't," replied Aqua, looking a little glum and handing the beautiful tiara back to the fairy. "I'm saving my pirate pennies for the Midsummer Fair."

"Good point," Marina said. "And we need to get on with returning the piddocks to the fairy who cursed us if there's to be any fair at all!"

The girls walked along the rows of shops

that were nestled in the cave walls along the base of the dome. They passed a bakery selling sugar sponge cakes and sea strawberry macaroons, and a chocolate shop selling treats made from the cocoa trees that grew in the dome. There was a shop with rails and rails of beautiful fairy skirts and gowns and another sold silken slippers decorated with sea anemones and seashells.

One shop in particular caught Marina's eye.

CARISSA'S
SEA~HERBS & REMEDIES
'WISE FAIRY'
Fortune Teller   Seeing Pool

"Perhaps we need a wise fairy to help us?" Marina suggested.

"Sea fairies with seeing pools are deeply respected in the fairy realm," said Aqua.

"It looks very dark and creepy in there," Oceana whimpered, glancing into the shadowy doorway. "Perhaps I'll just wait for you out here?"

"You're such a little worry whelk," giggled Aqua, taking Oceana by one hand as Marina took the other. "Let's go inside and try and sort this curse business out."

The girls stepped into the dark cavern and looked around, their eyes slowly adjusting to the dim light.

Hundreds of sparkling starfish hung from the ceiling on strings and the air was scented with sea spices. The walls were stacked with

turtle leather books, as well as jars and bottles containing powders and potions.

"Are you sure this 'wise fairy' isn't a witch?" muttered Oceana.

The girls giggled nervously as they waited for someone to appear.

Marina noticed a large counter at the back of the shop.

"Look over here," she whispered.

Sat on the counter top was a huge glass jar filled with water, and floating inside was a big spotted squid.

The three pirates leant in to have a closer look.

"Has it . . . ?" Oceana asked nervously.

"Passed on?" Aqua sniffed. "It looks that way – it's not moving and its eyes are closed shut."

"Poor thing," mused Marina as the girls gazed at the sea creature.

Suddenly the squid's large pink eyelids flashed open and glared right at them!

"Limpets!" Oceana gasped. "I thought you said it was perished!"

"I see you've met my little friend," came a kind voice from a curtain behind the counter. "I am Carissa, and this tentacled little chap is Star."

The girls stood in awe of the beautiful sea fairy that was now standing behind the counter. Her hair was the colour of crystal seas, and her eyes the colour of the desert island sand.

Purple and red fronds of seaweed were braided through her hair and her wings shimmered like the ocean at sunrise.

"Very pleased to meet you," Marina managed to blurt out. "I am Marina and these are my friends, Aqua and Oceana. We are the Petticoat Pirates from Periwinkle Lagoon."

"What a pleasure to meet such pretty pirates!"

Carissa smiled. "Now tell me, how can I help you?"

"Well," Marina

continued, "yesterday morning a swarm of angry sea fairies flew into our lagoon. They sprinkled sparkling powder over all the pirates and now the whole lagoon is hiccupping bubbles."

"Blue and green bubbles," Aqua added.

"Oceana examined the bubble slime and it seemed to contain piddocks," Marina said, pointing to their baskets of sea creatures.

"Mixed with blue branching seaweed," Aqua chirped in again.

"I see," Carissa frowned. "Piddocks do live above here, on the rocks around Whirlpool Gully, but it wouldn't be any fairy from this realm who cursed you . . . except . . ." Carissa paused for a moment. "There was once an old sea fairy who lived here called Ulvie. She disapproved of how we younger fairies were

running things in the dome and so she moved away, taking a tribe of tiny blue and green sea fairies with her."

"The fairies who came to the lagoon were blue and green," Marina said.

"And tiny," added Aqua, nodding her head enthusiastically.

"Limpets!" Oceana said under her breath.

"Where did Ulvie go?" asked Marina.

"She left through the long tunnels that surround our domed realm and has made her new home on rocks high up on the surface. And that's the only place where I know blue branching seaweed grows. I'm sure it is Ulvie who has cursed you." Carissa sighed. "Many a time we have tried to visit her and ask her to rejoin us but . . ." she trailed off.

"But what?" Marina gulped.

"She has a protector: a huge and angry crab that guards her lair. I think she used her magic to make the crab so big. No one has ever dared pass its snapping pincers."

The three Petticoat Pirates looked at one another.

"We must brave the crab and try and visit Ulvie. We have to ask her to lift the curse," said Marina.

"Take this potion with you," Carissa said, handing Marina a tiny blue bottle labelled INVISIBILITY POTION.

"We can't drink that, it's fairy food!" Aqua gasped. "We'll be forced to stay here in the realm for ever!"

"Trust me," Carissa replied, her sandy-coloured eyes looking straight into Aqua's. "I am here to help you, not trick you. This potion is for mortals like you. Sadly this kind of magic doesn't have any effect on fairies, so I can't use it myself to get past the crab."

Marina popped the bottle in the pocket of her petticoat and turned to face her friends.

"To the Petticoat Pirates," she said firmly, reaching out for her friends' hands.

As Carissa waved goodbye, the three pirates left Carissa's shop with the baskets of piddocks and the tiny bottle of potion, and made their way towards Ulvie's lair. Marina was determined to lead her pirates bravely, but her head was filled with thoughts of giant crabs, angry fairies and deep, dark tunnels.

Chapter Six

Once the girls had left the light and airy dome of the sea fairies, the tunnels seemed extra dark and scary.

"Urgh!" groaned Aqua as she squeezed through a particularly narrow passage. "I've got a sea anemone stuck in my hair!"

"Here, let me get that for you." Marina carefully pulled the dark red sticky little creature out of her friend's blonde locks.

"I didn't think the tunnels would be this

small and narrow," Oceana said, her legs aching from climbing up the steep passageway.

"Don't worry," Marina called from the front of the line, "I think it looks a bit wider ahead."

Sure enough the tunnel broadened quickly to reveal a vast cavern. Tiny shards of light streamed down from cracks in the ceiling.

"We must have climbed right up to the surface – that's the sky up there!" Oceana said. But her relief didn't last long. From a dark corner of the cavern came a scuttling, scratching sound.

"Limpets!" Oceana muttered, nearly dropping her basket of piddocks. "Is that what I think it is?"

"It's Ulvie's crab – quick, the potion!"

Marina said, taking a gulp from the bottle and passing it to Aqua.

"I'm not sure we should drink that potion!" Aqua said, studying the bottle in her hand. "What if Carissa is trying to trick us? She is a fairy after all!"

"I'm willing to take my chances," Oceana yelped, grabbing the glass bottle from Aqua and taking a large sip.

Just as the potion passed Oceana's lips, the giant crab spotted the girls with its beady black eyes. It started to move towards the girls, its enormous, pink pincers snapping closer and closer.

"Aqua, just drink it! You have no choice unless you want to end up as crab food!" Marina shrieked. She and Oceana were slowly beginning to fade as the potion began to take hold.

"Please, Aqua," Oceana begged her friend, pushing the bottle towards Aqua's mouth. "Please drink it." The little bottle now seemed to hover in mid-air as Oceana became invisible.

At last Aqua grabbed the bottle. "Well, here's to an eternity in the realm of sea fairies," she said, before swallowing the last of the potion.

"Please hurry up and work, please hurry up and work," Aqua said to herself. Her back was pressed against the damp cavern wall as the giant crab swung its enormous pincers right in front of her.

"Aqua! Run!" shouted Marina. "You're invisible now!"

As the crab's powerful pincer smashed into the cave wall, Aqua ducked and ran under the crab's legs.

"Where are you both? I can't see you!" Aqua shouted.

"Up here!" came two little voices from a ledge high up on the cavern wall.

Aqua could see the baskets of piddocks floating in the air. She climbed up the wall with her own basket and pushed herself on to the ledge. Slowly the three pirates became visible again.

"I think we're safe here," Marina said, looking down at the crab below them.

"But we still have to try and find Ulvie's lair." Oceana's voice wobbled as she spoke. "I don't know what's worse, giant crabs or angry fairies!"

"Look, maybe we can get through over there," Aqua said. She pointed at an opening in the cave wall further along the narrow ledge, which was just visible through a thick curtain of dark green seaweed. The girls edged their way along to the opening and pushed their way through into another tunnel.

"Bleurgh," Aqua spluttered, wiping fronds of slimy seaweed from her face. "This place is disgusting!"

"Don't worry, it seems drier here," Marina said, touching the walls of the tunnel. "We must be above sea level."

As they hurried along, it became lighter and lighter until they stepped out the other end into daylight.

"We're up on the rocks above Whirlpool Gully!" Marina gasped as she looked down at the whirlpools swirling in the sea.

"Look! There's Old Inky!" Aqua shouted, pointing to the huge circles of the whirlpool that had sucked them down the night before.

"I think I know where Ulvie might live," whispered a very stiff and frightened-looking Oceana.

The others turned to look where Oceana was pointing.

There, across the craggy rocks, stood a stone tower. Its grey walls were covered in blue branching seaweed. Tiny blue and green fairies

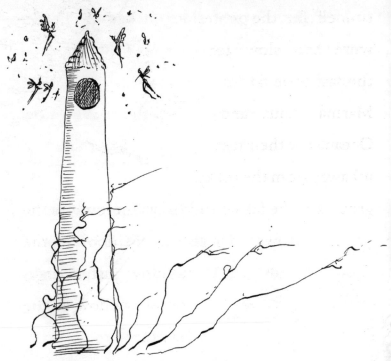

flitted around the tower's turret and the rocky garden was full of piddocks.

"Limpets," Oceana whimpered.

The tiny fairies must have spotted the pirates as they began to surge angrily towards the girls.

"Quick!" Marina cried. "Back to the

tunnel!" But the pirates were too slow for the fast little fairies. Marina, Aqua and Oceana felt their feet lift away from the rocky ground as the fairies carried them towards the tower. There was no door to the building, just a large, round window at the very top.

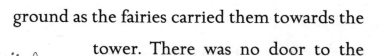

One by one the pirates were flown through the window – and the next thing they knew they were standing in front of a sea fairy with long blue hair and turquoise eyes. It had to be Ulvie!

"Aaaaah, pirates from Periwinkle Lagoon. I'm Ulvie. I've been expecting you!" The sea fairy spoke in a low, bubbling sounding voice. "Sit down, sit down." Ulvie gestured at three little chairs behind them, made from driftwood.

The girls sat down nervously, and Marina looked around the small circular room. In the centre was a rock pool, and the walls were lined with shelves – but they were empty apart from four or five green bottles, just to the right of Ulvie.

Ulvie slowly shuffled over to a large cooking range, her ragged green skirt dragging behind her. She stirred a big, black pot that bubbled away.

"PIDDOCK, ANYONE?" she suddenly snapped, her long, blue hair swirling as she turned around to face the girls with a cooked

squidgy thing stabbed on to the end of her spoon. "You like my piddocks, don't you? So much so you have stolen some from me!"

The girls were too terrified to move or speak at first. But Marina swallowed hard and stood up from her chair slowly, her legs feeling like eels in jelly.

"We're terribly sorry, Ulvie. The pirates who picked your piddocks didn't know they weren't supposed to take them. Here, look, we're returning them to you." Marina lifted her basket from the floor.

"SILENCE, pirate. Sit back down. I know why you're here. I've been watching you."

Marina, Aqua and Oceana looked at each other with their wide eyes as Ulvie shuffled to the rock pool. She swirled the clear water about with a gnarly hand.

"I can see all things in my seeing pool. I saw you coming. I can see those wretched fairies down in the dome. And I can see the monstrous crab they have sent to keep me up here and stop me returning to the fairy realm."

Marina summoned the courage to speak to the bitter old fairy again.

"Ulvie, the fairies in the dome think that the crab belongs to you, so that you can keep them out."

Ulvie's weather-worn face softened a little as she gazed out of her round window to the whirlpools beyond.

"I didn't like the way the younger fairies were doing things back at the dome. I am an old and wise fairy, but they wouldn't listen to me any more. They thought they knew better. I wanted a break so I gathered my potions and my fairy helpers." Ulvie gestured to the tiny fairies that were flitting around the room. "I came up here to teach the youngsters a lesson! To show them they needed to follow the old fairy ways. I thought that before long they would be begging me to return, but the dome fairies sent that crab to keep me here. I can never go home now."

Marina moved a little closer to Ulvie. "But the fairies under the dome want you to return.

83

They have tried to visit but, as I said, they think that YOU have put the crab there to keep them away."

"So if it's not your crab, and it's not their crab, whose crab is it?" Aqua asked, her forehead creasing in a frown.

"Ulvie," Marina continued, "do you want to return to the fairy realm?"

"Yes, I do, terribly. I have just five potions left now, and the only food to eat is piddocks. That was why I was so angry when your pirate fishermen took some away."

Oceana looked down at the baskets. She screwed her nose up and wondered how anyone could eat such ugly little things.

Marina gently took Ulvie's hand, realising that there had been a terrible misunderstanding. "If we helped you return to the fairy realm under the dome and get rid of that crab, would you lift the curse on Periwinkle Lagoon?"

Ulvie smiled a little. "Yes, yes, I'd be happy to, but I can't lift the curse on my own. I don't have all the sea herbs I need to make the antidote. I will need some of the plants grown in the dome, and Carissa's help, if she will give it to me . . ."

"Oh, I'm quite sure she will," Marina said as she helped Ulvie pack her last few potions into her bag.

"I'm looking forward to returning to the dome," Ulvie said. "I never much liked piddocks anyway!"

Ulvie flew out of the round window, and

the Petticoat Pirates were gently lifted down by the tiny sea fairies. Then they nervously made their way back through the tunnels towards the giant crab's cavern.

Chapter Seven

Soon the group arrived at the ledge above the crab's cavern and watched the huge pink creature snapping its pincers at them.

"How do you go about catching a giant crab?" Marina wondered aloud.

Oceana rummaged around in her petticoat pockets and pulled out a fine net. "We could use this?" she said.

"I am amazed at what you manage to fit in your petticoats!" laughed Aqua. "You are truly ready for anything!"

"Even giant crabs," Marina said, winking.

"Will that fine net be strong enough to hold such a big crab?" Ulvie asked.

"It's strong enough to tow a whale from the southern seas! I've tested it myself," Oceana replied proudly.

"OK, so how are we going to get the net over the crab?" Marina asked. "We're too high up here."

Oceana looked at Ulvie. "Would you mind if we borrowed your little fairy friends?" she asked.

Ulvie quickly summoned the tiny blue and green sea fairies to her, and Oceana gave each of the fairies part of the edge of the net.

"Now fly over that crab and drop the net!" she told them. "We'll climb down and secure it."

The fairies flew with the net outstretched, and quickly dropped it on the crab. Meanwhile, Marina, Aqua and Oceana climbed down the rocks and ran to tie the net up at the bottom. The captured crab wriggled and snapped his pincers but he couldn't escape.

Marina stared up at his big, black eyes protruding out the top of his pink body.

"Look," she said, "I think the crab is . . . "

"Crying!" Aqua finished.

Big, salty tears were plopping down on to the cavern floor and the crab began to wail.

"Wa ha, waaaaaa haaa haaaa," sobbed the crab. "Please don't hurt me!"

"You can speak?" Oceana said in amazement.

"Yes, I'm sorry. I didn't mean to scare you earlier. I was only trying to talk to you and then you all disappeared."

The girls and Ulvie all looked at one another, not quite sure how to deal with an upset crab.

"What are you doing here?" Marina finally asked.

The crab sniffed. "I used to be a carrier crab, down in the dome. I loved my job, gathering all the seaweed and sea flowers for the fairies' potions."

"But you're so big!" Oceana said as she carefully unfastened the net.

"I wasn't always this big," the crab replied. "I was delivering some seaweed to Carissa, and she had made a yummy soup. I didn't think she'd mind if I had a quick taste... I was so hungry after a long day of work."

"Something tells me it wasn't ordinary soup!" said Aqua.

"No, it wasn't soup at all, it was a growing potion. I started to get bigger, and bigger, and bigger, so I scuttled away into this cave to hide. But now I'm too big to leave it!"

"Ulvie," Marina said, "will any of your potions help?"

"As fairy luck would have it, I think I have just the thing!" Ulvie reached into her bag and pulled out a bottle labelled "shrinking potion." Ulvie passed the little bottle to her tiny fairy helpers who flew above the giant crab and sprinkled the potion over his big, pink back.

Marina, Aqua, Oceana and Ulvie watched as the crab creaked and squeaked and slowly shrank back down to his original size. It was quite a sight!

"This place truly is magical," Oceana said.

"Oh, thank you!" the crab said – with a much higher voice than before.

Marina bent down and scooped up the now hand-sized crab. "I think it's high time you were returned to your carrying duties," she said, looking into his beady eyes.

"Carissa will be so cross with me," he whimpered.

"You just have to tell the truth, little crab. I'm sure Carissa will forgive you," Marina replied.

"Come on, everybody!" Aqua shouted impatiently from further down the tunnel. "Let's get back to the dome."

Steadily the group made their way down through the dark tunnels, hoping that Carissa would not only forgive the crab, but help them mix a cure for the hiccups in Periwinkle Lagoon.

Chapter Eight

Rays of pink evening sunlight streamed down through the surface of the sea and into the dome as the tired group came out from the tunnels.

"What a beautiful sunset!" Oceana sighed, looking around the fairy dome.

Strings of starfish draped from the ceiling of the dome began to glow, and fairies flitted around the caves lighting little lamps.

The scent of delicious fairy meals filled

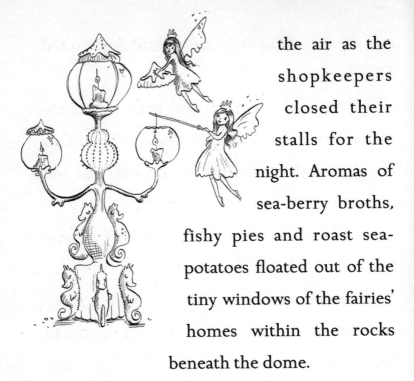

the air as the shopkeepers closed their stalls for the night. Aromas of sea-berry broths, fishy pies and roast sea-potatoes floated out of the tiny windows of the fairies' homes within the rocks beneath the dome.

"We should hurry! We need to get there before Carissa goes home," Marina said as they hurried through the fairy crowds.

"Phew!" Aqua sighed as they came close. "Carissa's shop is still open."

"Wait," Ulvie said, hesitating at the entrance. "What if Carissa doesn't want to see me?"

Marina, Aqua and Oceana huddled around Ulvie.

"Just remember it's all been a terrible misunderstanding," Marina said. "Tell her that the giant crab was nothing to do with you and everything will be just fine, I promise."

Marina passed the crab to Ulvie. "Our new friend will help you to explain!"

Ulvie took a deep breath. "I'll go in first," she said, gently holding the little pink crab in her hands.

The Petticoat Pirates stood back and watched as Ulvie stepped inside, her ragged green skirt trailing behind her.

"I truly hope that Ulvie and Carissa can be friends again," Marina sighed. "Ulvie has had a hard time up in that tower."

"And *I* truly hope that Ulvie and Carissa

can concoct a potion to cure Periwinkle Lagoon's hiccups!" Aqua said.

As they waited, the Petticoat Pirates gazed up at Ulvie's tiny fairy friends. They were flying around with the other sea fairies under the dome.

"Look how happy they are! It's wonderful to see them all together again," Oceana said, smiling.

"I think we can go in now," Marina said as she took a quick peek through the window. "It looks like Ulvie and Carissa are friends once more!"

The girls entered the little shop as Ulvie and Carissa hugged and laughed together.

"Oh, pirates," Carissa gushed, "thank you for bringing our friend Ulvie back to us and unravelling the mystery of the 'giant' crab."

Carissa was holding the very sheepish-looking crab in her hand.

"Carissa?" Marina said anxiously. "We were wondering if you might be able to help us ... "

"Of course, Marina. Anything for my new pirate friends."

"Well," Marina continued, "do you remember we told you of the curse at Periwinkle Lagoon?"

Ulvie looked very guilty and embarrassed. "It was me, I'm afraid. I was angry that the pirates had stolen my piddocks. There was nothing else to eat up on the rocks – they were all I had."

Carissa put her arm around Ulvie. "It must have been incredibly difficult for you living up there." She paused and looked at the pirate girls. "I'm so glad you brought Ulvie back home. But what can we do about the hiccupping at Periwinkle Lagoon?"

"Ulvie has some of the special sea herbs that will help make up the antidote, but it must be mixed with certain plants that only grow here," Marina said, looking out of the shop door at the lush gardens under the dome.

Carissa smiled knowingly. "I think you need to go and do some fetching," she whispered to the little crab. She put him down on the ground and watched him scuttle off sideways out of the shop. Moments later he returned, carrying a few fronds of red seaweed on his back.

"I think these might be what you're looking for," squeaked the crab.

"Oh, well done!" Carissa said, bending over to pick them up. "These are just what we need to mix with Ulvie's sea herbs to complete the antidote."

Ulvie and Carissa crushed the sea herbs and the red seaweed together in a pestle and mortar until a runny purple paste formed. Then the two fairies decanted the gloop into a tiny bottle and popped a cork in the top.

"There," Carissa declared proudly. "One antidote for a hiccupping curse."

"Limpets," Oceana muttered to herself.

"What is it, my young pirate?" asked Carissa. "Is there something wrong?"

"Possibly," Oceana replied. "You see, this is a very small bottle of potion, and there are hundreds of hiccupping pirates at Periwinkle Lagoon."

"Oh dear," Carissa said. "But we don't have enough ingredients to make much more."

"What are we going to do?" Aqua cried, her eyes filling with tears. "We're still going to have to call off the fair!"

"I have an idea," Marina said, raising her eyebrow. "How much potion do we need to cure one pirate?"

"Just the tiniest drop," replied Carissa. Ulvie nodded alongside her.

Marina pointed to Carissa's large oven and the jars of sea wheat flour and sea crystal sugar on the shelves.

"Let's make COOKIES," she said. "We can

mix the antidote into the cookie dough. We'll make enough cookies to feed all the pirates!"

"What a marvellous idea," said Carissa.

Marina bent down to talk to the little crab. "Can you go and see if the fairy chocolatier will open up her shop for us? We're going to need a lot of chocolate drops!"

The tiny crab scuttled off again.

Aqua still looked worried. "But we can't ask the pirates to eat fairy food, Marina, remember! We know how dangerous it is. What if they all get sucked down into the fairy realm for ever?"

Ulvie chuckled. "Don't worry, my lovely Petticoat Pirate, let me share a fairy secret with you: as long as the food has left the fairy realm, it can't harm you. I promise."

Aqua smiled with relief. The girls began to

measure out the flour and the sea crystal sugar, while Carissa lit her oven.

Ulvie fetched a large seashell bowl and put it on the counter.

Carissa mixed the flour, the sea crystal sugar and the antidote, before adding a little butter.

"We're just waiting for the chocolate drops now!" Marina said.

"Where has that little crab got to?" Aqua asked.

But before anyone could answer, the crab scuttled back through the door, followed by scores of other carrier crabs. They all carried bags of chocolate drops on their backs!

"I asked my friends to help me carry these," smiled the crab. He looked happy to be back with his fellow carrier crabs again.

They added the chocolate drops, and Marina helped Carissa roll out the cookie dough. Then Aqua and Oceana used a starfish-shaped cutter to stamp out the little biscuits and Ulvie popped the cookies in the oven.

They waited patiently as the cookies baked, the sweet smell making the Petticoat Pirates rather hungry. When they were ready, Carissa set them out to cool and then Marina decorated them with pink sugar crystal. Finally, Aqua packed all the cookies into a sea straw basket – they were ready!

"We should hurry," Marina said. "We need to get back to Periwinkle Lagoon as quickly as possible."

"But we can't go back the way we came!" Oceana shuddered just thinking about being sucked down Old Inky.

"We know how you can get safely back

to the sea," said the little carrier crab. "Follow us."

The pirates hugged Carissa and Ulvie.

"Thank you for all your help," Marina said.

"No, it is I who must thank you," Carissa said. "You have returned our friend Ulvie to us."

Ulvie stepped forward and took the girls' hands.

"Thank you for forgiving me. I'm sorry I cursed your lagoon. And thank you for bringing me back to the dome and to my fairy friends – I've been lonely for so long."

The girls hugged Ulvie again and then waved goodbye as they followed the long line of tiny pink crabs through the tunnels and back to *The Petticoat*.

Chapter Nine

Back at the cavern, Marina, Aqua and Oceana waded through the water and climbed up on to *The Petticoat*, putting the basket of cookies safely in the cabin. The ship looked like it had been fixed and tidied by the kind fairies.

"Now what?" Aqua said, looking around her. "We can't go back up Old Inky!"

The Petticoat began to judder.

"Hold on tight!" Marina cried. "I think something's happening!"

The girls grasped the rails of the ship as it slowly began to spin around and around.

"Urgh," Oceana groaned, "I feel sick!"

The ship began to lift up in the air. Marina looked above them – where Old Inky had been swirling was now open sky!

"This place is certainly magical," Marina gasped.

"How are we flying?" Aqua said as the little ship spun higher and higher.

"Look!" Oceana cried.

The girls looked to where Oceana was pointing, at the sides of *The Petticoat*. All of Ulvie's little blue and green fairies were carrying the ship up into the air, their pretty wings fluttering in the shimmering evening light.

The beach in the cavern grew smaller

and smaller below them. It was lined with the carrier crabs all waving their pincers.

"Wave at our crab friends," Marina said.

As the fairies flew *The Petticoat* up into the sky, the sea closed around the cavern again. The surface of the water began to slowly swirl back into the shape of Old Inky.

"So that's how you get in and out of the sea fairy realm!" Aqua said, holding on to her hat to stop it from blowing away.

The fairies carried the ship a safe distance away from Whirlpool Gully and then gently lowered *The Petticoat* back down on to the sea. They all waved before flying off and disappearing down Old Inky.

The girls stood on the deck, peering down to see if they could spy the fairy dome beneath

the sea, but it was well hidden below the whirlpools and waves.

"The sea fairy realm was such a magical and wonderful place to be," said Marina, taking the wheel of *The Petticoat* and turning the ship towards home.

"It was certainly a bit different to Periwinkle Lagoon!" Aqua said, hoisting the sails.

"Shame there's no easier way in and out!" said Oceana, moving towards the hatch to the cabins. "Now I think we all deserve a cup of kelp tea."

"Lovely!" Marina and Aqua called back in unison.

"The weather seems favourable," Marina said, listening to the wind as it talked to her. "We should make it back to Periwinkle Lagoon by dawn. Just in time for the fair!"

The girls changed into warm, dry clothes and began their journey back home to the lagoon, armed with their cargo of chocolate cookies.

Chapter Ten

As *The Petticoat* neared Periwinkle Lagoon, the sun was just peeping up over the horizon.

"There are lots of trading ships making their way here already," Oceana said, peering out to the seas around the lagoon with her telescope.

"We need to dish out those antidote cookies faster than a flying fish!" Aqua said. "If our visitors see we've been cursed they'll turn their ships right around and go home!"

"Quick," Marina said, "let's head straight to the flagship. Captainess Periwinkle can raise the calling flag and we can get everybody cured."

Captainess Periwinkle was waiting for the girls on the deck of her ship.

"My fine little . . . hic . . . Petticoat Pirates," she cried. "What news do you have? Did you find an antidote for the . . . hic . . . curse?"

"We did, Captainess," Marina said, looking proudly at her friends. "Together we had quite an adventure!"

"You must tell me all about it later," the Captainess said. "The sea traders are a-coming and . . . hic . . . we still have a lagoon full of hiccupping pirates."

Marina handed the Captainess one of the starfish-shaped cookies.

"This is delicious," said the Captainess. She

finished chewing and took a deep breath. "My hiccups have stopped!" She called over two of the Flagship's senior pirates: "Raise the calling flag, and sound the calling horn as well. We have to summon every last pirate to this ship as quickly as possible!"

Very quickly the flagship filled up with hiccupping pirates, as bubbles floated and popped about everywhere.

Marina, Aqua and Oceana handed a cookie to each pirate. Slowly but surely, calm and peace settled on the lagoon once again. No more hiccups. No more bubbles.

"May the Midsummer Fair at Periwinkle Lagoon commence!" cried the Captainess, her sword held high in the air.

The lagoon was a flurry of activity as the visiting ships drew nearer. Floating stalls were

set up all around the flagship and the pirates laid out their wares to sell.

Soon, many hundreds of ships had arrived from all over the vast seas. Sea traders from the southern seas brought spices and sea berries. The ships from the northern seas brought ice creams and sea ice diamonds. The fairies from the Sea Lavender Islands brought perfumes and soaps. The mermaids from Starfish Reef arrived with fresh food from their mer-farms.

It seemed like every sea creature imaginable was rowing their boat, riding their seahorse or swimming around the lagoon, stocking up on things for the months ahead.

Meanwhile, Captainess Periwinkle stood on the deck of the flagship with the three Petticoat Pirates.

"You have made me as proud as a pufferfish once again!" she gushed, brushing some leftover bubble slime from her stripy bodice and long red skirt.

"We were happy to help," Marina said, taking Aqua and Oceana's hands.

"Not as happy as I am with my new sea diamond spangle boots," Aqua said, sticking one sparkling boot out from under her petticoats.

Captainess Periwinkle held her sword in the air. "May the Petticoat Pirates prevail!" she shouted.

"May the Petticoat Pirates prevail," the

three friends whispered to one another. They grasped each other's hands, remembering their adventures in Whirlpool Gully, the land of the sea fairies.

"Until our next adventure?" Marina said. She passed around a plate that held the last of the cookies.

"Until next time," Aqua and Oceana replied, biting into their fairy snacks and smiling.

The End

Ship's Log

Now that you've learnt all about Marina,
Aqua and Oceana, why not read on to see
how you can have a Petticoat Pirate
adventure of your own!

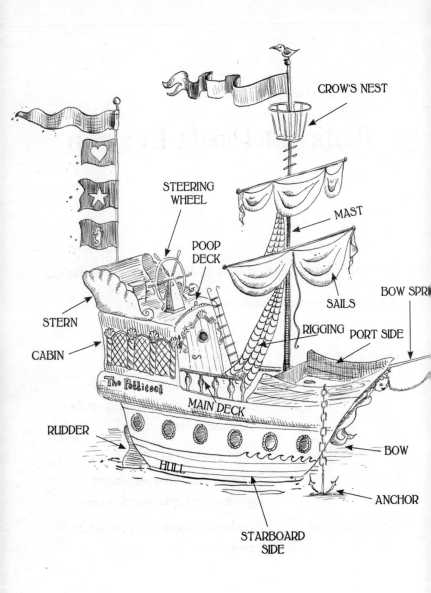

CROW'S NEST

STEERING
WHEEL

POOP
DECK

MAST

SAILS

BOW SPR

STERN

RIGGING   PORT SIDE

CABIN

The Petticoat

MAIN DECK

RUDDER

BOW

HULL

ANCHOR

STARBOARD
SIDE

Petticoat Pirate Lexicon

Would you like to speak like a proper Petticoat Pirate? Of course you would!

Captainess	*The queen of the pirates*
Cargo	*The objects a ship carries in its hold – such as items to trade at the Midsummer Fair*
The fairy realm	*All the places fairies live*
Flagship	*The most important ship in the lagoon – the Captainess lives here*
Hoist the sails!	*Put the sails up so we can go on an adventure!*

Jumping jellyfish!	*This is what you say when you're very surprised by something*
Kelp flakes	*Delicious breakfast cereal*
To perish	*Eek! This is what would happen if you'd been gobbled by a shark ...*
Pirate pennies	*Money*
Port	*Left*
Sea crystals	*Sugar*
Starboard	*Right*
A seeing pool	*Fairies use these to have a sneaky peek at what other people are doing*
A worry whelk	*A pirate who gets worried about things easily*

May the Petticoat Pirates prevail!

We wish the Petticoat Pirates strength and success!

Starfish Biscuits for Hungry Pirates

Please remember that you will need an adult's help with this, especially because ovens get very hot! The Petticoat Pirates like to wear aprons when they cook at home, maybe you would too.

Ingredients

For the biscuits

- 250g plain flour
- 85g caster sugar
- 175g unsalted butter, at room temperature, cubed

For the icing

- 250g white icing sugar
- red and yellow food colouring
- edible glitter

What to do

1. Heat oven to 180C/fan 160C/gas mark 4.

2. Put the sugar and butter into
   a bowl and use a spoon
   to mix them together.
   Then add the flour a
   little at a time. First, the
   mixture will form crumbs,
   and then it should stick
   together into one big ball.

3. Spread a large sheet of baking parchment
   over your work surface and put the dough
   onto it. Dust with a little flour, then roll out
   to about half a centimetre thickness. Stamp
   out star shapes using a star cutter. Carefully
   peel the rest of the dough away from the
   stamped stars. Lift stars on the baking

parchment onto a baking tray and get an adult to put them in the oven. Cook for 10-15 minutes until they are a pale golden colour.

4. Cool the biscuits on a wire rack.

5. Split the icing sugar between three bowls and mix a little water in to each one to make a paste. Add a drop of yellow food colouring to one bowl, red to another and a drop of yellow and red to make orange in the third bowl. Spoon over your star-shaped biscuits, then sprinkle on your edible glitter.

You will have red, orange and yellow starfish biscuits that sparkle!

Spot the Fairy Difference

There are five differences between these two beautiful fairies – can you spot them all?